For Gregory:
Love,
Uncle Billy
Aunt Dona
May 1981

Scuffy the Tugboat

Scuffy
THE TUGBOAT
and His Adventures Down the River

by Gertrude Crampton
illustrated by Tibor Gergely

gb® GOLDEN PRESS
Western Publishing Company, Inc.
Racine, Wisconsin

SCUFFY THE TUGBOAT, originally published and still avail-
able as a Little Golden Book, has delighted youngsters for more
than twenty-five years. This classic story by Gertrude Crampton
is presented here in a new, larger edition, with the colorful artwork
of Tibor Gergely.

Fourth Printing, 1976

GOLDEN, A GOLDEN BOOK®, SCUFFY THE TUGBOAT, and GOLDEN PRESS®
are trademarks of Western Publishing Company, Inc.
No part of this book may be reproduced or copied in any form
without written permission from the publisher.
ISBN 0-307-10490-7

Scuffy was sad.

Scuffy was cross.

Scuffy sniffed his blue smokestack.

"A toy store is no place for a red-painted tugboat," said Scuffy, and he sniffed his blue smokestack again. "I was meant for bigger things."

"Perhaps you would not be cross if you went sailing," said the man with the polka dot tie, who owned the shop.

So one night he took Scuffy home to his little boy.
He filled the bathtub with water.

"Sail, little tugboat," said the little boy.

"I won't sail in a bathtub," said Scuffy. "A tub is
no place for a red-painted tugboat. I was meant for
bigger things."

The next day the man with the polka dot tie and
his little boy carried Scuffy to a laughing brook that
started high in the hills.

"Sail, little tugboat," said the man with the polka
dot tie.

Scuffy floated on a ruffle of the brook and saw
above him the smiling faces of the man with the
polka dot tie and his little boy.

It was Spring, and the brook was full to the brim with its water. And the water moved in a hurry, as all things move in a hurry when it is Spring.

Scuffy was in a hurry, too.

"Come back, little tugboat, come back," cried the little boy as the hurrying, brimful brook carried Scuffy downstream.

"Not I," tooted Scuffy. "Not I. This is the life for me."

All that day Scuffy sailed along with the brook.

Past the meadows filled with cowslips. Past the women washing clothes on the bank. Past the little woods filled with violets.

Cows came to the brook to drink.

They stood in the cool water, and it was fun to sail around between their legs and bump softly into their noses.

It was fun to see them drink.

But when a white and brown cow almost drank Scuffy instead of the brook's cool water, Scuffy was frightened. That was not fun!

And there was no rest. For it was Spring, and the brook moved in a hurry, as all things move in a hurry when it is Spring.

Night came, and with it the moon.

There was nothing to see but the quiet trees.

"This is nice," thought Scuffy. "I like night."

Suddenly an owl called out, "Hoot! Hooot!"

"Toot, tooot!" cried the frightened tugboat, and he wished he could see the smiling face of the man with the polka dot tie.

When morning came and the sun danced on the brook again, Scuffy was cross instead of frightened.

"A brook is no place for a red-painted tugboat," said Scuffy. "I was meant for bigger things."

Around a bend and past a small woods the brook ran, and there was another brook.

"Oh, oh!" said Scuffy. "What happens now? Which way do I want to go?"

But there was only one way to go, and that was with the running water where the two brooks met.

He was proud when he sailed past villages.
"People build villages at the edge of my river,"
said Scuffy, and he straightened his blue smokestack.
Once Scuffy's river joined a small one jammed with
logs. Here were men in heavy jackets and great boots,

walking about on the floating logs, trying to pry them free.

"Toot, toot, let me through," demanded Scuffy. But the men paid no attention to him. They pushed the logs apart so they would drift with the river toward the sawmill in town. Scuffy bumped along with the jostling logs.

"Ouch!" he cried as two logs bumped together.

"This is a fine river," said Scuffy, "but it's very busy and very big for me."

He was proud when he sailed under the bridges.

"My river is so wide and so deep that people must build bridges to cross it."

The river moved through big towns now instead of villages.

And the bridges over it were very wide—wide enough so that many cars and trucks and streetcars could cross all at once.

The river got deeper and deeper. Scuffy did not have to tuck up his bottom.

The river moved faster and faster.

"I feel like a train instead of a tugboat," said Scuffy, as he hurried along.

He was proud when he passed the old sawmill with its water wheel.

But high in the hills and mountains the winter snow melted. Water filled the brooks and rushed from there into the small rivers. Faster and faster it flowed, to the great river where Scuffy sailed.

"There is too much water in this river," said Scuffy, as he pitched and tossed on the waves. "Soon it will splash over the top, and what a flood there will be!"

Soon great armies of men came to save the fields and towns from the rushing water.

They filled bags with sand and put them at the edge of the river.

"They're making higher banks for the river," Scuffy shouted, "to hold the water back." The water rose higher and higher.

The men built the sandbags higher and higher. Higher! went the river. Higher! went the sandbags.

At last the water rose no more. The floodwater rushed on to the sea, and Scuffy raced along with the flood. The people and the fields and the towns were safe once again.

On went the river to the sea. At last Scuffy sailed into a big city. Here the river widened, and all about were docks and wharves.

Oh, it was a busy place and a noisy place! The cranes groaned as they swung the cargoes into great ships. The porters shouted as they carried suitcases and boxes on board.

Horses stamped and truck motors roared; street-cars clanged and people shouted. Scuffy said, "Toot, toot," but nobody noticed.

The whistles blew—policemen's whistles, train whistles, deep whistles from the great ships as the gangplanks were pulled in.

And just beyond lay the sea.

"Oh, oh!" cried Scuffy when he saw the sea. "There is no end to the sea. I wish I could find the man with

the polka dot tie and his little boy!"

Just as the little red-painted tugboat sailed past the last piece of land, a hand reached out and picked him up. And there was the man with the polka dot tie, with his little boy beside him.

Scuffy is home now with the man with the polka dot tie and his little boy. He sails from one end of the bathtub to the other.

"This is the place for a red-painted tugboat," says Scuffy. "And this is the life for me."